LITTLE MISS CONTRARY
all in a muddle

Original concept by Rog
Illustrated and written by A

MR. MEN   LITTLE MISS

Now, Little Miss Contrary lives in a place called Muddleland.

In Muddleland, hens live in cow barns, which works.

And cows live in chicken coops, which doesn't work!

Muddleland suits Little Miss Contrary down to the ground, or up to the sky, as they say in Muddleland.

When she goes into the butcher's and asks for apples the butcher gives her a loaf of bread!

Which is what she had wanted all along.

Not so very long ago Little Miss Contrary was having breakfast, at lunchtime, when the telephone rang.

Little Miss Contrary went to the front door, but of course there was no one there.

The phone rang again. She picked it up. The wrong way round. "Goodbye!" she shouted.

Everyone in Muddleland has to shout when they use the phone.

It was Mr Muddle.

Now you would think Mr Muddle also lived in Muddleland, wouldn't you?

But he doesn't.

He wanted to, but got muddled-up and bought a house on the coast near Seatown.

However, each year he goes to Muddleland for his holidays and stays with Little Miss Contrary.

"I'd simply hate for you to come and stay. I'll see you last week."

"Hello!" finished Miss Contrary, and hung up.

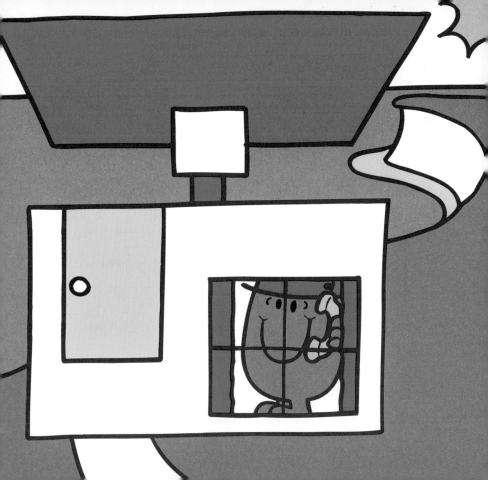

Little Miss Contrary looked around her.

"This house needs a good autumn-clean," she said to herself.

And, of course, what she meant was that her house needed a good spring-clean.

She polished the carpets and hoovered the beds!

And she scrubbed the television and washed the plants!

In the middle of all this scrubbing and polishing and washing, Little Miss Contrary saw a cat.

Little Miss Contrary is terrified of cats.

Well, she isn't called Miss Contrary for nothing, is she?

With an 'EEEEK!' she leapt on to a stool.

Poor Little Miss Contrary.

She was too frightened to get down off the stool.

And there she stayed.

All night long.

The next morning there was a knock at the door.

"Go away!" called Little Miss Contrary, meaning 'Come in'.

Luckily it was Mr Muddle on the other side of the door, so in he went.

"Oh, don't help me!" cried Little Miss Contrary. "There's a cat loose in the house!"

Mr Muddle understood completely.
"I don't know what to do," he said, and left.

What he meant was that he did know what to do.

And in no time at all he returned with a mouse.

And the mouse, being a Muddleland mouse, chased the cat out of the house.

Little Miss Contrary made a saucer of tea and she and Mr Muddle settled down for a chat.

A chat that is much too muddling to write down here, and anyway, it's getting late now, and it's time to switch off the light and go to sleep.

Well it isn't really, but that is what Little Miss Contrary would have written if she was writing this story, but luckily she isn't.

You see, Little Miss Contrary gets everything the wrong way round.

She turns her lights off when it gets dark ...

... and turns them on when she goes to bed!

Good morning!

3 Great Offers for MR. MEN Fans!

MR. MEN TOKEN

1 New Mr. Men or Little Miss Library Bus Presentation Cases

A brand new stronger, roomier school bus library box, with sturdy carrying handle and stay-closed fasteners.

The full colour, wipe-clean boxes make a great home for your full collection.

They're just £5.99 inc P&P and free bookmark!

☐ MR. MEN ☐ LITTLE MISS (please tick and order overleaf)

2 Door Hangers and Posters

In every Mr. Men and Little Miss book like this one, you will find a special token. Collect 6 tokens and we will send you a brilliant Mr. Men or Little Miss poster and a Mr. Men or Little Miss double sided full colour bedroom door hanger of your choice. Simply tick your choice in the list and tape a 50p coin for your two items to this page.

PLEASE STICK YOUR 50P COIN HERE

Door Hangers (please tick)
☐ Mr. Nosey & Mr. Muddle
☐ Mr. Slow & Mr. Busy
☐ Mr. Messy & Mr. Quiet
☐ Mr. Perfect & Mr. Forgetful
☐ Little Miss Fun & Little Miss Late
☐ Little Miss Helpful & Little Miss Tidy
☐ Little Miss Busy & Little Miss Brainy
☐ Little Miss Star & Little Miss Fun

Posters (please tick)
☐ MR. MEN
☐ LITTLE MISS

3 Sixteen Beautiful Fridge Magnets – any 2 for £2.00!
inc.P&P

They're very special collector's items!
Simply tick your first and second* choices from the list below
of any 2 characters!

1st Choice
- [ ] Mr. Happy
- [ ] Mr. Lazy
- [ ] Mr. Topsy-Turvy
- [ ] Mr. Bounce
- [ ] Mr. Bump
- [ ] Mr. Small
- [ ] Mr. Snow
- [ ] Mr. Wrong

- [ ] Mr. Daydream
- [ ] Mr. Tickle
- [ ] Mr. Greedy
- [ ] Mr. Funny
- [ ] Little Miss Giggles
- [ ] Little Miss Splendid
- [ ] Little Miss Naughty
- [ ] Little Miss Sunshine

2nd Choice
- [ ] Mr. Happy
- [ ] Mr. Lazy
- [ ] Mr. Topsy-Turvy
- [ ] Mr. Bounce
- [ ] Mr. Bump
- [ ] Mr. Small
- [ ] Mr. Snow
- [ ] Mr. Wrong

- [ ] Mr. Daydream
- [ ] Mr. Tickle
- [ ] Mr. Greedy
- [ ] Mr. Funny
- [ ] Little Miss Giggles
- [ ] Little Miss Splendid
- [ ] Little Miss Naughty
- [ ] Little Miss Sunshine

*Only in case your first choice is out of stock.

--- TO BE COMPLETED BY AN ADULT ---

To apply for any of these great offers, ask an adult to complete the coupon below and send it with the appropriate payment and tokens, if needed, to MR. MEN OFFERS, PO BOX 7, MANCHESTER M19 2HD

- [ ] Please send _____ Mr. Men Library case(s) and/or _____ Little Miss Library case(s) at £5.99 each inc P&P
- [ ] Please send a poster and door hanger as selected overleaf. I enclose six tokens plus a 50p coin for P&P
- [ ] Please send me _____ pair(s) of Mr. Men/Little Miss fridge magnets, as selected above at £2.00 inc P&P

Fan's Name _____

Address _____

_____ **Postcode** _____

Date of Birth _____

Name of Parent/Guardian _____

Total amount enclosed £ _____

- [ ] **I enclose a cheque/postal order payable to Egmont Books Limited**
- [ ] **Please charge my MasterCard/Visa/Amex/Switch or Delta account** (delete as appropriate)

Card Number

Expiry date ___/___ **Signature** _____

Please allow 28 days for delivery. We reserve the right to change the terms of this offer at any time but we offer a 14 day money back guarantee. This does not affect your statutory rights.

MR.MEN   LITTLE MISS
Mr. Men and Little Miss™ & ©Mrs. Roger Hargreaves

CUT ALONG DOTTED LINE AND RETURN THIS WHOLE PAGE